Our Neighbors

An Imprint of Pop!
popbooksonline.com

SOMALI AMERICANS

by Elizabeth Andrews

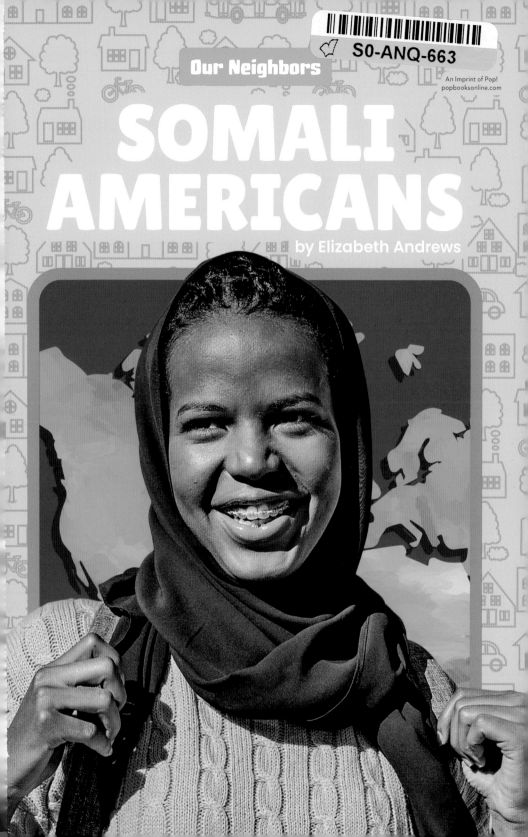

abdobooks.com

Published by Pop!, a division of ABDO, PO Box 398166, Minneapolis, Minnesota 55439. Copyright ©2022 by Abdo Consulting Group, Inc. International copyrights reserved in all countries. No part of this book may be reproduced in any form without written permission from the publisher. DiscoverRoo™ is a trademark and logo of Pop!.

Printed in the United States of America, North Mankato, Minnesota.

052021
092021

 **THIS BOOK CONTAINS RECYCLED MATERIALS**

Cover Photos: ASSOCIATED PRESS, Shutterstock Images

Interior Photos: REUTERS/Alamy Stock Photo, 5; Ken Hawkins/Alamy Stock Photo, 7; Shutterstock Images, 9, 22–23, 26; iStockphoto, 10–11, 13, 15, 16, 21, 24–25; Authenticated News/Staff, 18 (top); John Moore/AP/Shutterstock, 18 (bottom left); DAI KUROKAWA/EPA-EFE/Shutterstock, 18 (bottom right); Ignelzi/AP/Shutterstock, 19 (top); Preston Ehrler/SOPA Images/Shutterstock, 19 (bottom); Lenny Agencja Fotograficzna Caro/Alamy Stock Photo, 28–29

Editor: Tyler Gieseke
Series Designer: Laura Graphenteen
Library of Congress Control Number: 2020948846
Publisher's Cataloging-in-Publication Data
Names: Andrews, Elizabeth, author.
Title: Somali Americans / by Elizabeth Andrews
Description: Minneapolis, Minnesota : Pop!, 2022 | Series: Our neighbors | Includes online resources and index.
Identifiers: ISBN 9781098240066 (lib. bdg.) | ISBN 9781644946008 (pbk.) | ISBN 9781098240981 (ebook)
Subjects: LCSH: Somali Americans--Juvenile literature. | Ethnicity--United States--Juvenile literature. | Neighbors--Juvenile literature. | Immigrants--United States--History--Juvenile literature.
Classification: DDC 973.004--dc23

WELCOME TO DiscoverRoo!

Pop open this book and you'll find QR codes loaded with information, so you can learn even more!

Scan this code* and others like it while you read, or visit the website below to make this book pop!

popbooksonline.com/somali-americans

*Scanning QR codes requires a web-enabled smart device with a QR code reader app and a camera.

TABLE OF
CONTENTS

CHAPTER 1

CELEBRATING SOMALIA

The street outside Jennah's apartment building was busy with activity for days. Her neighbors helped put up tents and fences. Her dad checked things off

WATCH A VIDEO HERE!

People sing, dance, and celebrate together during Somali Week. It is a joyful time.

a clipboard. Everyone she knew had

worked hard. They were getting ready for

Somali Week of Minnesota.

The light blue of Somalia's flag was everywhere Jennah looked now. She walked down the street with her mom. When they dressed that morning, they put on blue hijabs to match their flag. Tonight, Somali Week would begin with a celebration of Somali Independence Day. As they headed toward the stage, they stopped at their friend's tent for cardamom cookies.

Somali families are close and happy like many American families.

Jennah knew the week showed Somali culture through food, arts, and entertainment. There would be speeches, music, and dancing. Jennah was most excited for the dancing. She loved watching all the older girls in beautiful dresses perform onstage. She hoped to do the same when she was their age.

CHAPTER 2

HOMELAND

Somalia is located in the Horn of Africa.

This is an important location. It sits

right on the edge of Africa and below

southwest Asia.

LEARN MORE HERE!

MAP OF SOMALIA

ERITREA

DJIBOUTI

disputed boundary

Somaliland

Puntland

N
W E
S

ETHIOPIA

Indian Ocean

disputed boundary

SOMALIA

WHERE IN THE WORLD?

Mogadishu

Somalia's leader was removed from power in 1991. Then, different groups started claiming power over parts of Somalia. None of these regions are official. That's why the borders are labeled "disputed."

The people of Somalia live in clans

around the country. Some Somalis

are traveling farmers. They move their

The northern part of Somalia is hilly. The southern part is flat and dry.

animals to find grasses to eat. Somalia

also has a good fishing **industry** and

urban areas.

In the 1900s, Somalia was under the control of European governments. The country gained its independence in 1960. For a while the country was peaceful. But in 1969 General Mohamed Siad Barre took over. Barre was not a good leader. Dangerous **civil wars** broke out between different clans.

DID YOU KNOW? A new government in 2012 brought some peace to Somalia. The world supported the new government.

Refugee camps are crowded and often lack clean water and food.

During the civil wars, large groups **immigrated** to the United States as **refugees**. They wanted a safer home. Minnesota has the largest Somali American population.

CHAPTER 3

FINDING COMMUNITY

To escape the **civil wars**, Somalis **immigrated** to the United States. Many had seen movies set in America. They knew it as a safe and happy country. They hoped to experience that for themselves.

COMPLETE AN ACTIVITY HERE!

Some families immigrate for new and better opportunities.

Most Somali Americans arrived as

refugees. They did not have a lot of

money or things. The US government

The United States offered a place for young Somalis to be themselves.

gave them money and helped while they looked for housing, schools, and jobs. The government also helped decide where in the states the immigrants would live.

Minnesota ended up with the most Somali Americans in the country. The state has good chances for jobs and education. Once some refugees started settling in Minnesota, others came too. The refugees formed a strong community. It became the safe and comfortable place Somali refugees had been looking for.

SOMALI IMMIGRATION TIMELINE

1960

Somalia gains independence from Europe. The United Republic of Somalia is born.

1969

Mohamed Siad Barre takes over. The country becomes more dangerous for its citizens.

1990s-2005

The largest flow of Somali **refugees** comes to the United States.

2012

A new Somali government declares power, hopefully bringing peace.

1991

General Barre is taken out of power. There are still **civil wars** between clans trying to earn total power.

2019

Ilhan Omar becomes the first Somali American member of Congress.

CHAPTER 4

TWO DIFFERENT CULTURES

Many Somali American children struggle to understand where they belong. They are living as a mix of two very different cultures. Somali Americans live and act

LEARN MORE HERE!

It's fun and important to be friends with people different from you!

as everyone else to fit in with their friends.

They listen to popular music and wear

trendy clothes.

They may act more traditional when they're home with their families. They'll treat their older family members with respect. They may work harder to follow Muslim culture and beliefs at home.

The tall towers of mosques play an annoucement saying it's time for Muslims to stop and pray.

A place that Somali Americans might find it easiest to be just as they are is at a **mosque**. There, Somali Americans can be with people who share similar experiences.

It's normal to see young girls with baseball hats over their hijabs. They run to the park with their friends. They will play tag or shoot hoops with their crushes on the basketball court. They head home for supper just like every other kid on the playground.

DID YOU KNOW? Nike sells hijabs made out of athletic material so girls can play sports comfortably.

Somali American kids have all kinds of hobbies.

Somali American kids will settle back
in with their family once they get home.

Sambusa *is a fried pastry. It can have all kinds of filling. The most common is beef.*

Their mothers will often cook dinner for the family. Dinners are usually spiced rice, meat, and vegetables. During meals, families can come together and enjoy classic parts of Somalia.

SOMALI MALLS

Somali Malls are places that bring Somali culture to American neighborhoods. Malls like Little Mogadishu in Minnesota serve as community centers. They mix Somali art, food, friendship, and business. People can have traditional food like sambusas and chai teas. **Henna** artists can put their designs on shoppers. And shopkeepers sell beautiful and unique clothes.

Somalis did not come to the United States with many physical possessions. But they brought their strong traditions. Most Somali Americans are Muslim. This has allowed them to create tight-knit communities based in their culture and beliefs. Somali Americans started mixing those into everyday American life. A fantastic combination of both places is the result.

Some people might move back to Somalia when it's safe. For now, they are happy in the United States.

MAKING CONNECTIONS

TEXT-TO-SELF

If you went to visit a Somali mall, what would you want to see? What food would you try?

TEXT-TO-TEXT

Have you read other books about immigrants in America? What do they have in common with this title? How are they different?

TEXT-TO-WORLD

Somali Week celebrates Somali culture through food and art. Are there any other cultural celebrations that you can think of? What is the culture like? What sort of events take place?

GLOSSARY

civil war — a war between people from the same country.

henna — a semipermanent tattoo drawn on with reddish brown dye.

immigrate — to enter another country to live. A person who immigrates is an immigrant.

industry — businesses that make goods or provide services.

mosque — a building for Muslims to worship in.

refugee — a person who flees to a new country to escape danger.

urban — related to a city or downtown area where lots of people live and work.

INDEX

ONLINE RESOURCES
popbooksonline.com

Scan this code* and others like it while you read, or visit the website below to make this book pop!

popbooksonline.com/somali-americans

*Scanning QR codes requires a web-enabled smart device with a QR code reader app and a camera.